Adapted by Shirley Brown

Illustrations by Henry Markowitz

ALL RIGHTS RESERVED, INCLUDING THE RIGHT
TO REPRODUCE THIS BOOK OR PORTIONS
THEREOF IN ANY FORM.

PUBLISHED SIMULTANEOUSLY IN CANADA
BY COLUMBIA RECORDS OF CANADA LTD.

LIBRARY OF CONGRESS
CATALOG CARD NUMBER: 68-8910

Copyright © 1968 by CBS Records		Printed in U.S.A.

# Cinderella

Once upon a time in a far-off kingdom there was a beautiful girl named Cinderella who lived with her step-mother and her two step-sisters.

Horribella and Terribella. The two step-sisters were selfish, greedy and mean, especially to Cinderella. They made her do all the housework.

They gave poor Cinderella orders all day long! Cinderella never complained because she was so sweet. She cleaned the rooms and made the beds, washed the dishes, scoured the pots, dusted the furniture and scrubbed the floors. She worked and worked and worked and worked.

Cinderella was so tired that she just fell asleep by the stove in the kitchen, and warmed herself by the cinders. That is why she was called Cinderella.

In the kingdom where Cinderella lived, there was a palace on top of a hill, and in this palace, there lived a real Prince, with his parents, the King and the Queen.

The Prince was a very handsome young man, and the time had come for him to choose a wife. So the King and Queen planned for weeks and weeks to give a huge party, a ball, and all the young ladies from the noblest families in the kingdom were invited.

Naturally, the palace had to be fixed up for the ball. All the servants were put to work, polishing the silver, and shining the crystal.

Now, Horribella and Terribella, Cinderella's step-sisters, got invitations to the ball, but Cinderella did not get an invitation.

And how they teased her, and teased her! They showed her the new dresses they were going to wear. They made her do extra work. And still Cinderella did not complain, because she was so sweet. "Wouldn't you like to go to the ball?" they asked Cinderella.

"Oh, yes, I would!" cried Cinderella. "Hah! You can't go to the ball! You didn't get invited!" screamed Horribella. "Hmm! You can't go. You haven't even got a dress!" yelled Terribella.

Poor Cinderella held back her tears, and she thought to herself, "At least I can dream of going to the ball. I can still dream."

Horribella and Terribella were extra mean to Cinderella because they could not fit into their new dresses and had to go on a diet.

The day of the grand ball arrived.
The two step-sisters took five hours to get dressed.

"Get my bracelets, Cinderella!"
"Hurry, hurry Cinderella! Help me into this dress!"

And they didn't stop their teasing.

And, finally, Horribella and Terribella squeezed into their hired coach, and away they went to the ball, leaving Cinderella to clean up the mess they made getting dressed.

Cinderella was very sad. She watched until the carriage was out of sight. Then she just sat down and cried. Big tears rolled down her cheeks.

Suddenly, Cinderella heard a strange sound. The air near her shimmered with all the colors of the rainbow.

"Who are you?" cried Cinderella.

"I am your fairy godmother."

"Fairy godmother?" Cinderella looked puzzled.

"Yes, I am your fairy godmother. Would you like to go to the ball?"

"Oh, are you going to tease me, too?" cried Cinderella, and she started to cry again.

"I think I can arrange for you to go. But I can't do everything. You've got to help yourself a little."
"Now, if you really want to go to the ball, there's work to be done!"
"I'll do anything you say!" said Cinderella, and she smiled!

"Pumpkin! I need a pumpkin!"
Cinderella ran into the garden and brought a pumpkin.
"Set it on the ground, and stand back!"

A touch of the wand, 🎵 and the pumpkin turned into a beautiful coach!
"Mice! I need some mice!"
Cinderella brought her seven pet mice and 🎵 one-two-three-four-five-six, there were six beautiful horses to pull the coach!

There was still one fat mouse left in the cage.
"Oh, he'll be lonely, all alone," said Cinderella, who was always considerate of others. "Couldn't you make him . . . something?"

That was easy. The fat mouse became a roly-poly coachman with a large moustache. Some footmen were needed for the coach. "Cinderella, there is a family of lizards in the watering-can near the potted plants by the back door. They can be footmen!"

Presto! Six elegant footmen bowed low, and took their places on the carriage.

Cinderella's ragged dress became a radiant, long evening gown of gold and silver, frosted here and there with exquisite little gems. Even Cinderella's hair was done in the latest style.

"Now hurry, Cindrella, and have a lovely time."
"I hope I'm not being too much trouble," said Cinderella, "but I don't have any shoes."

That was no trouble 🎵 and a pair of tiny glass slippers appeared on Cinderella's feet.

"Cinderella, my dear, the magic will last only until midnight."
"Oh, that's all right, Fairy Godmother," said Cinderella. "I'm so happy that I'm going at all."

"But remember, at midnight, everything will change back. Then your coach will turn to a pumpkin, the horses and coachman to mice, the footmen to lizards and your fine clothes to rags. Have a very good time, but remember, be back before midnight. You must remember this."

Cinderella was so happy that she hardly heard. Her lovely eyes were shining with excitement as she climbed into the carriage. "Good-bye! Good-bye! Thank you! Goodbye!"
And the roly-poly coachman cracked his whip, and away went Cinderella to the ball!

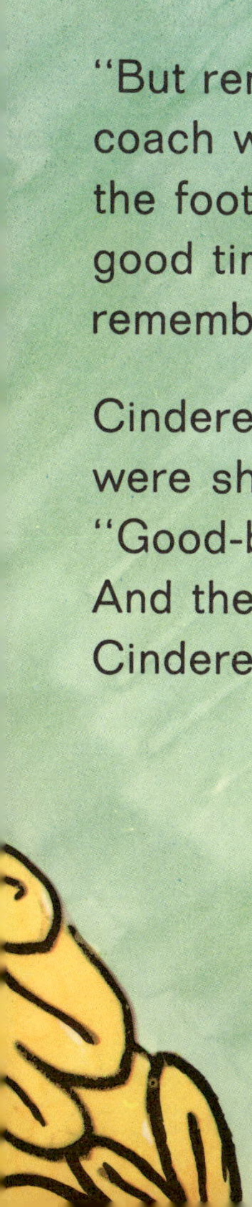

The palace was lit with thousands of lights.
There were hundreds and hundreds of guests.

And the Prince had met many, many young ladies, all wanting to be the new Princess. But the Prince hadn't found one that he specially liked. Suddenly, there was a buzz of conversation about the magnificent carriage which had arrived, and the beautiful young girl who was getting out of it.

The Prince dashed down the palace steps to greet her himself.

As Cinderella turned to go up the steps, she saw the handsomest man she had ever seen standing in front of her.

And the Prince found himself looking at a girl who took his breath away. They stood and looked at each other for what seemed a long, long time. Then the Prince slowly took Cinderella's hand and led her up the steps of the palace and into the grand ballroom and they started to dance.

Everyone else stopped dancing. Even the orchestra stopped playing. Everyone stared, but Cinderella and the Prince kept dancing.

The orchestra leader coughed and waved his baton. The orchestra started playing again. Cinderella was so beautiful that evening that Horribella and Terribella, her two step-sisters, didn't even recognize her.

"Please tell me your name," asked the young Prince, again and again. But Cinderella was afraid to say her name. So she only smiled. And they danced and they danced.

Suddenly, it was midnight. As the clock began to strike twelve, Cinderella remembered! She turned and ran out of the ballroom.

own the palace steps, she ran, and she was in such a hurry that even when ne of her glass slippers fell off she didn't stop to pick it up.

t the last stroke of midnight, everything changed back, and Cinderella, now n her ragged dress, still running, disappeared into the night.

The Prince ran up to the palace gate. There was no one there, except the gatekeeper. "Have you seen a beautiful Princess go by?" he asked.

"No, your highness," replied the gatekeeper, "only a poor girl dressed in rags. She was carrying a pumpkin and the strangest thing was that some mice and lizards followed her."

The Prince went sadly back up the palace steps. Why had the Princess run away? Then he saw the one glass slipper that Cinderella had lost lying on the steps. He picked it up and looked at it. "I will find her," he thought to himself, "I will find her if it takes forever."

Finally Cinderella reached home, exhausted, and began to clean up the mess her two step-sisters had left behind them when they got dressed for the ball. She was still cleaning when Horribella and Terribella got back.

"Well, you missed it. All I can say is, you missed it," said Horribella.

"There was this girl, she must have been a Princess, nobody knows from where, and she ran from the ball at midnight, and she dropped this glass slipper, and the Prince, they say, is in love with her!" said Terribella.

"You missed it. All I can say is, you missed it," said Horribella.

And the two step-sisters went to bed. Cinderella smiled to herself.

The Prince, determined to solve the mystery and find the girl of his dreams, had his herald issue a proclamation.

And the Prince wondered if he would find his true love again.

From house to house went the King's messengers, trying the glass slipper on every young girl in the kingdom.

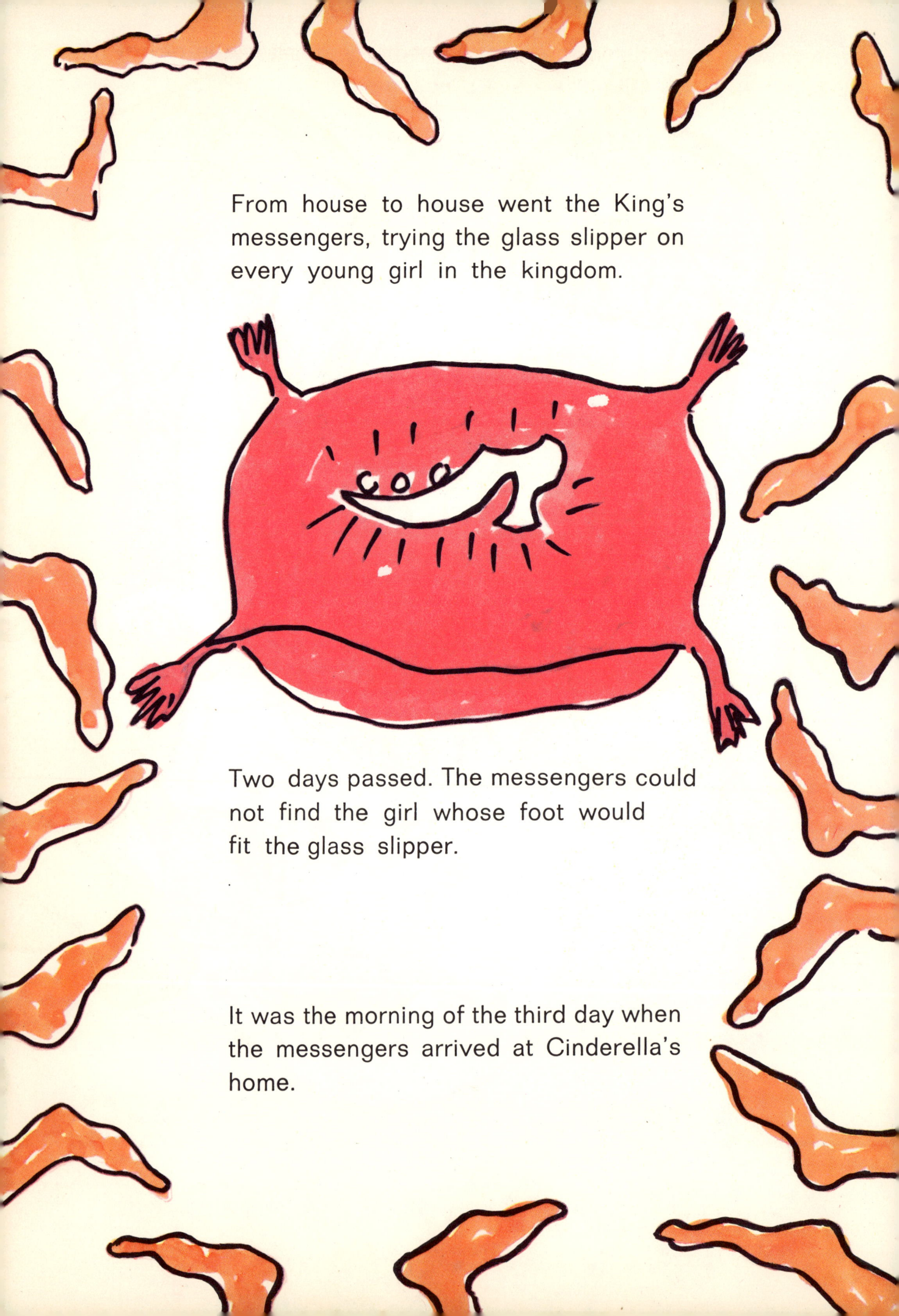

Two days passed. The messengers could not find the girl whose foot would fit the glass slipper.

It was the morning of the third day when the messengers arrived at Cinderella's home.

"Me first! Me first!"
screamed Terribella.
"No, me! Me!" screamed Horribella,
and pushing Terribella out of the way, she tried to put her foot in the
glass slipper.

"Ladies, please!" said the King's messenger. Of course neither of the
step-sisters could get so much as a big toe in the tiny slipper,
let alone a foot.

"Are there any other young ladies in the house?" asked the King's messenger. "No!" said Horribella and Terribella, but then the King's messenger noticed Cinderella standing behind the stove. "I have been given orders," said the King's messenger "to try the slipper on every maiden in the the kingdom.

Will you please come forward, Miss?"
"She doesn't count," said Terribella.
"She's no Princess!" cried Horribella.
But by that time Cinderella was wearing the tiny glass slipper. It fit perfectly.

"Congratulations, Miss," said the King's messenger. "It looks as if you're the Princess we have been trying to find, although," and he scratched his head, looking at Cinderella's dirty clothes, "I don't see how you can come to the palace, dressed as you are."

Then, suddenly, Cinderella's Fairy godmother appeared and with a touch of her wand, 🎵 Cinderella was dressed in a gown more dazzling than the one she had worn to the ball.

Then Horribella said, "Oh, sorry, Cinderella." And Terribella started to cry and said, "Oh, I'm sorry, Cinderella." Both step-sisters started to cry and blow their noses. Cinderella looked at them. She was so happy she just couldn't be angry.

So she said, "That's all right, Horribella and Terribella." And she told her sisters she wanted them to be her friends forever. Cinderella was driven to the castle in the royal carriage.
The Prince was waiting to greet her.

The King ordered that a grand celebration be held in honor of his son's marriage to Cinderella. From that day on the castle was filled with music and laughter and the Prince and Cinderella lived happily ever after.